A delightful picture book for young children that illustrates familiar everyday objects.

Encourage your child to talk about the objects, and ask simple questions such as ''What colour is this?'' and ''Where do we find this?'' The most important thing is to make looking at the book fun for both of you!

Each illustration contains something yellow (the yolk in the picture of the egg, for example). Point these out to your child as you look at the pictures together. Then ask him or her to find the yellow section in each picture.

The blue, red, and green picture books in this series may also be used in similar ways.

Acknowledgment:
The publishers would like to thank Maureen Hallahan for the hand lettering used in this book.

British Library Cataloguing in Publication Data
Baby's yellow picture book.
1. English language. Words—Illustrations—
For children
I. Dillow, John
428.1'022'2
ISBN 0-7214-1100-2

First edition

Published by Ladybird Books Ltd Loughborough Leicestershire UK
Ladybird Books Inc Auburn Maine 04210 USA

Printed in England

Baby's
YELLOW
picture book

illustrated by JOHN DILLOW

Ladybird Books

horse

plane

lemon

butterfly

strawberries

frog

egg

pram

penguin

wellingtons

bucket
and spade

shells

truck

watch

television

mouse

plant

shirt

elephant

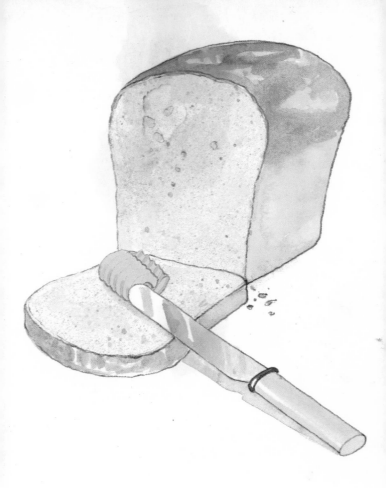

bread

flowers

crayons

camera

drum